Days of the week

With Macy

Written and Illustrated By:
Christine Kuschewski

Love Queen

LET YOUR LOVE SHINE THROUGH

"Mom, can you teach me about the days of the week today? Remember when you taught me the months of the year, you said you would teach me?" asked Macy.

"Yes, Macy, I will teach you," replied her mom.

"You already know there are 12 months in a year. Each month is made up of weeks, and each week has 7 days," explained Macy's mom.

SUNDAY

Every week starts with Sunday.
Macy likes to watch football on
Sunday!

MONDAY

Monday is the second day of the week. This is the start of the school and work week. Macy misses her mom when she goes to work on Monday.

TUESDAY

The third day of the week is Tuesday. Macy calls this "two for day" because she likes to get 2 treats on Tuesday.

WEDNESDAY

The fourth day of the week is Wednesday. Many people call this "hump day" because it is the middle of the week. Macy walks with mom on Wednesday.

THURSDAY

Thursday comes next. Macy enjoys snuggling with her mom after she gets home from work on Thursday.

FRIDAY

Finally it is Friday. This is the last day of school and work for most people. Macy is excited because her mom will be home for the next 2 days!

SATURDAY

The last day of the week is
Saturday. Macy plays with her
friends on Saturday.

Saturday and Sunday are called the weekend.

SATURDAY
SUNDAY

Monday, Tuesday, Wednesday, Thursday and Friday are called week days.

"My favorite days are Saturday and Sunday," said Macy.
"Why is that?" asked her mom.
"You don't have to go to work. That means I get to be with you all day!" said Macy excitedly.
"My favorite day is any day I get to spend with you, Macy" her mom replied.

Macy's World Titles

Christine Kuschewski has been a special education teacher for 22 years. She loves teaching children how to read. Her love for books and education has led her to writing children's books. Christine and Macy live in Arizona. Macy loves to spend time with her best friends, Toby, Kona and their family. Macy is a 7 year-old Bichon Frise, Poodle, Maltese and Shih-Tzu mix. Everyone who meets Macy falls in love with her. Together Christine and Macy enjoy spreading love to the world.

Made in the USA
Middletown, DE
21 October 2022

13168361R00018